Do these activiti...
your child to rea...

D0790853

See It, Say It

Ask your child to color the star beside the word when he or she finds it in the book.
Make sure your child understands what each word means.

⭐ sheep ⭐ tomatoes

⭐ carrot ⭐ dreams

Add It UP

Read each word in the list below to your child.
Help your child count how many times she or he sees that word in the book.

| Chapter 1 | Chapter 2 | Chapter 3 | Chapter 4 |
| give, gave | stay, save | loves, have | worship, cares |

To, With, and By

To	Read four pages out loud *to* your child. Run your finger under the words as you say them at a normal speed. Make sure your child is looking at the words.
With	Read the same four pages out loud *with* your child. Run your finger under the words as you say them at a normal speed. Your child will probably say every other word correctly.
By	Run your finger under the words as your child says them *by* himself or herself. Help your child fix any mistakes.

Continue doing *To, With, and By* a few pages at a time for the rest of this book. Have your child reread this story for the next several days until it sounds great and is practically memorized.

 Go to www.RocketReaders.com for more reading tips.

Faith Kidz® is an imprint of Cook Communications Ministries
Colorado Springs, Colorado 80918
Cook Communications, Paris, Ontario
Kingsway Communications,
Eastbourne, England

WHO CARES?
©2003 by Cook Communications

First printing, 2003
Printed in Korea
1 2 3 4 5 6 7 Printing/Year 07 06 05 04 03

Senior Editor: Heather Gemmen
Design Manager: Jeffrey P. Barnes
Designer: Paul Segsworth

Who Cares?

Rocket Readers Level 4

Written by
Heather Gemmen
and
Mary McNeil

Illustrated by
John Taylor

Chapter 1

Genesis 4

Cain
(Kayn)
Abel
(Ay-buhl)

"God loves me!" said Abel.
"Who cares?" said Cain.

"God did not give me sheep.
God did not give me goats.
God did not give me cows."

"God gave me weeds.
God gave me rocks.
God gave me bugs."

"God gave me sheep.
God gave me goats.
God gave me cows.

I will give God the best sheep.
I will give God the best goat.
I will give God the best cow."

"I will give this corn.
I will give these carrots.
I will give these tomatoes.
Who cares?"

"I care," said God.

Chapter 2

Genesis 27

Jacob
(Jay-kuhb)
Esau
(Ee-saw)

"God loves me!" said Jacob.
"Who cares?" said Esau.

"Dad loves me.
Dad will give me everything.
I will have it all.

Mom loves you.
Mom can't give you anything.
You will have nothing at all."

"God loves me.
God will give me everything.
I will have it all.

I will have riches.
I will have many children.
I will have power," said Jacob.

"Who cares?" said Esau.

"I care," said God.

Chapter 3

Genesis 37

Joseph
(Joe-suhf)

"God loves me!" said Joseph.
"Who cares?" said his brothers.

"You will stay here.
No one will save you.
Your dreams will not come true."

"Will I stay here?
Will God save me?
Will my dreams come true?"

"You will not stay here.
You will go there.
Your dreams will not come true.
Who cares?" said his brothers.

"I care," said God.

Chapter 4

Matthew 4

Jesus
(Jee-sus)

"God loves me!" said Jesus.
"Who cares?" said Satan.

"All this is mine.
It can be yours.
Worship me."

"I will not worship you.
I will worship God."

"Who cares?" said Satan.

" I care," said God.

Faith Parenting Guide
Level 4 Reader
Reverence

Who Cares?

Life Issue: I want my child to know God wants the best we have.
Spiritual Building Block: Reverence

Do the following activities to help your child grow in reverence for God.

 Sight: Ask your child to bring you three of his or her belongings that are the "best."
Help your child understand that God gives us everything we have, especially the "best" things.
God wants us to give him the best we can, too, with our attitudes and praise.

Sound: Ask your child to give endings to these sentences:
Joseph's brothers threw him in a _____.
God cared for Abel, Joseph, and _____.
I know that God cares for me. That makes me feel
_____.

Touch: Have your child write these Bible words from Psalm 5:7 in the lines below.

In reverence I will bow down.